ZIGBY™
DIVES IN

BRIAN PATERSON

Collins

An imprint of HarperCollins*Publishers*

Have you read all the books about Zigby?

Zigby Camps Out
Zigby Hunts for Treasure
Zigby and the Ant Invaders
Zigby Dives In

For William, Charles and Henry

This edition produced for The Book People Ltd.,
Hall Wood Avenue, Haydock, St. Helens, WA11 9UL

First published in hardback in Great Britain by HarperCollins Publishers Ltd in 2003
First published in paperback by Collins Picture Books in 2004

1 3 5 7 9 10 8 6 4 2

ISBN: 0-00-776987-3

Collins Picture Books is an imprint of the Children's Division,
part of HarperCollins Publishers Ltd.

Text copyright © Alan MacDonald, Brian and Cynthia Paterson and HarperCollins Publishers Ltd 2003
Illustrations copyright © Brian Paterson 2003

Text by Alan MacDonald

ZIGBY™ and the Zigby character logo are trademarks of HarperCollins Publishers Ltd.

The HarperCollins website address is: www.harpercollinschildrensbooks.co.uk

Printed and bound in Thailand

Follow the winding stream to the
edge of the jungly forest and meet...

ZIGBY THE ZEBRA
OF MUDWATER CREEK.

Zigby the Zebra loves being outdoors, getting up
to mischief with his good friends, Bertie and McMeer.
There are always exciting new places to explore
and wonderful adventures waiting to happen
but sometimes he can't help trotting
straight into trouble!

Meet his friend, the African guinea fowl, **Bertie Bird**.
He's easily scared and thinks his friends are far too
naughty...but he'd hate to miss the fun, even if it does
mean getting dirty feathers!

McMeer is the cheeky little meerkat who
loves showing off and playing tricks. His practical
jokes sometimes cause all sorts of problems,
but he always knows how to have fun!

DOWN AT MUDWATER CREEK, ZIGBY WAS PLAYING
BASKETBALL WITH HIS FRIEND, BERTIE BIRD.
"I'm tired of being the basket," complained Bertie.
"Can't we do something else?"

"Yes, we can!" exclaimed McMeer,
arriving with his new fishing net.
"Watch me catch some fish!"

But the Creek was almost dry.

"Yuk!" said McMeer.

"Nothing but weedy muck!"

"We need deeper water," said Zigby.

"I know, let's go on a fishing trip!"

The friends set off through the forest to look for water. They took everything they might need on a fishing trip. Suddenly McMeer spotted a yellow butterfly. "Watch me catch it in my net!" he shouted.

He ran ahead, but tripped on a rock and tumbled
out of sight.
"Heeelp!" cried McMeer.
"Are you all right?" asked Bertie, peering down
through the bushes.
"Yes!" McMeer called. "Come and see what I've found!"

Zigby and Bertie clambered down some hidden steps, after McMeer. Through the trees they could see a curve of blue water sparkling in the sun.
"A hidden lagoon!" said Zigby.
"Perfect for fishing!"

"There's no one else here," said Bertie.
"Are you sure it's safe?"
"Of course it is!" scoffed McMeer.
"And I bet it's teeming with fish."

"I'll soon find out," said Zigby, putting on his trunks.
"I'm going in for a swim." Zigby waded into the lagoon.

"It's lovely and warm! Come in, Bertie!" he called.
"No fear," Bertie replied. "I don't like water. I'm going
  to build a sandcastle."

McMeer tied a hammock between two trees.
"This is the way to fish," he sighed, contentedly.
He waited a long time but nothing swam into
his net. After a while the warm sunshine made
him drowsy and he dozed off.
Then…

McMeer woke up with a start.

"Hey! Who took my fishing net?"

Bertie looked up. "You were asleep, McMeer!
You must have dropped it in the water."

McMeer started to cry. "I waaaant my fishing net!"

"Don't worry," said Zigby. "I'll dive down and find
it for you."

"Thanks," sniffed McMeer.

"Be careful, Zigby," warned Bertie.

Zigby dived down.
The water was clear and blue.
Shoals of tiny fish swam past
and a jellyfish wobbled by.

"McMeer's fishing net
must be on the bottom,"
thought Zigby. "There it
is, tangled in that
pink seaweed!"

Zigby grabbed the fishing net and pulled.
To his surprise the seaweed pulled
back! Two bulging eyes snapped
open and glared.
"Help! It's not seaweed, it's a
giant octopus!" thought Zigby.

Back on the beach, Zigby's friends were waiting for him. "He's been down there a long time. I hope he's all right," worried Bertie.

"And I hope he's got my fishing net!" added McMeer.

Zigby *had* got the fishing net.
But the octopus wasn't ready to give it back!
It chased Zigby in and out of the rocks.

Zigby swam through an arch, but the giant octopus squeezed through after him. He had to think of something fast. At that moment some striped fish swam by.

Zigby hid in the middle of them.
"Thanks, fish!" said Zigby.
"The octopus won't
see me in here!"

Finally, Zigby kicked up towards the surface.
He emerged from the water, gasping for breath,
but still holding McMeer's fishing net.

"Hooray! You've got it!" said McMeer.
"What took you so long?"
"There's a…huge…octopus down there," panted Zigby.
"With eight legs and big bulgy eyes?" asked Bertie.
"Yes," said Zigby. "How did you know?"

Zigby, Bertie and McMeer ran from the beach. They crashed through the trees and didn't stop running until they were home at Mudwater Creek.

"I'm never, ever, going back there again," vowed Bertie.
"Never mind," said Zigby. "At least we've still got
McMeer's fishing net. It's a pity we stepped on the
pole though."

McMeer examined the net sadly.
"And the net's ripped, too," he said.
"It's no use with a hole in the bottom."
Zigby had an idea. "Yes, it is!" he said.
"It's perfect for…